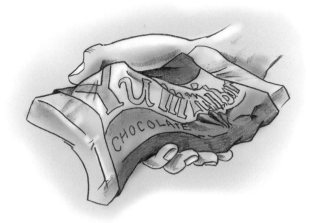

LOONIVERSE
MELTDOWN MADNESS

BY **DAVID LUBAR**

ILLUSTRATED BY
MATT LOVERIDGE

BRANCHES
SCHOLASTIC INC.

Read all the LOONIVERSE books!

 #1

 #2

 #3

#4

table of contents

FOR BARRY AND CAROL STOLTZE, WHO LIVE DOWN SOUTH, WHERE ALL THE CHOCOLATE MELTS.—DL

Library of Congress Cataloging-in-Publication Data

Lubar, David.

Meltdown madness / by David Lubar ; illustrated by Matt Loveridge.

p. cm. — (Looniverse ; 2)

Ever since Ed found the magic coin called Silver Center, strange things keep happening around him, but maybe if he finds the right words he can use the magic to raise money for the soccer team.

ISBN 978-0-545-49604-9 (pbk.) — ISBN 978-0-545-49603-2 (hardback) — ISBN 978-0-545-49686-5 (ebook)

1. Coins—Juvenile fiction. 2. Magic—Juvenile fiction. 3. Money-making projects for children— Juvenile fiction. [1. Coins—Fiction. 2. Magic—Fiction. 3. Moneymaking projects—Fiction.]

I. Loveridge, Matt, ill. II. Title.

PZ7.L96775Mel 2013

813.54—dc23

2012035573

ISBN 978-0-545-49603-2 (hardcover) / ISBN 978-0-545-49604-9 (paperback)

Text copyright © 2013 by David Lubar.

Interior illustrations copyright © 2013 by Scholastic Inc.

12 11 10 9 8 7 6 5 4 3 2 1   13 14 15 16 17 18/0

Printed in China   38

First Scholastic printing, July 2013

Illustrated by Matt Loveridge

Book design by Liz Herzog

ZOOM!
BOOM!

"I'm picking chocolate," I said to my friend Moose as we stood in line on Friday afternoon at the school gym. We'd gone there to sign up for the soccer team. We had to sell either chocolate bars, wrapping paper, or mixed nuts to raise money for our team uniforms.

Anyone who didn't raise the money couldn't play. But I wasn't worried. I figured I could sell all my chocolate this weekend.

"I'm going to pick wrapping paper," Moose said. "All my relatives will buy wrapping paper. They need tons of it."

"What for?" I asked.

"To wrap all the presents they give me," he said.

"My relatives give me socks," I said. "They don't need a lot of paper to wrap socks. What they need is a better idea of what to buy me."

PHHFFFWWWEEE!

Our soccer coach, Mr. Netz, blew his whistle. Then he said, "Listen up. You're here because you want to be on the soccer team, right?"

We all nodded.

"Team players need to show up to practice on time, and follow the rules," he said. "That takes responsibility. So does this." He started handing out the boxes.

"I'll take chocolate," I told Mr. Netz when I reached the front of the line.

"Good choice," he said. He handed me a big box. "Here you go. Thirty bars. Everyone loves chocolate."

"I'll take wrapping paper," Moose said.

"Good choice," Mr. Netz said. He handed Moose a big box, too. "Here you go. Thirty rolls. Everyone loves wrapping paper."

Then Moose and I left the gym. As we stepped outside, I realized picking chocolate was a big mistake.

"When did it get hot?" I asked. The air had been so cool this morning, I'd grabbed a jacket before I walked to school. Now the sun was blazing. This wasn't good. The heat would melt the chocolate. On top of that, unlike Moose's box of wrapping paper, my box was heavy.

Moose's older brother, Mouse, walked over to us from the playground. "Hey, that's a pretty big box. Want me to run it home for you?" he asked.

MOUSE

"Sure, thanks," I said. Mouse is really strong and fast. He could get the box to my house before the chocolate melted.

The sun burned down on us. The air grew even warmer. "Hurry," I said as I handed Mouse the box. "Go as fast as possible!"

An instant after the words left my mouth, I knew I'd made another mistake. And this one was enormous.

A gigantic blast knocked Moose and me off our feet as Mouse zoomed away.

"Uh-oh . . ." I said as I landed hard on my butt — and on the magic coin I always kept in my pocket. Mouse was already out of sight.

Little puffs of smoke rose from the ground along his path. "Come on!" I said to Moose as I leaped to my feet and started running. I had a feeling I'd better get home right away.

chapter 2

FOLLOW THAT TRAIL

As Moose and I ran to my house, I thought about my words. I'd told Mouse to "go as fast as possible." I had to learn to be more careful what I said. Strange things had been happening around me ever since I'd found a magic coin called the Silver Center.

THE SILVER CENTER

9

MR. SAGE

Mr. Sage, a store owner who was pretty strange himself, seemed to know a lot about the magic coin. He told me I had to give this coin to the Stranger. But it turned out *I* was the Stranger. So I ended up giving this coin to myself. Now, as the Stranger, I had the power to make strange things happen. Sometimes strange things even happened when I wasn't trying to make them happen.

I slowed down to catch my breath.

"Hey, Moose, how fast is 'as fast as possible'?" I asked.

"Just below the speed of light," Moose said. He's super smart. "About 186,000 miles a second. That's way faster than a rocket ship."

I remembered seeing a video of a rocket coming back to Earth. It had gotten *really* hot.

I noticed a patch of grass by the curb that was smoking and smoldering. This was looking worse and worse. I ran faster. We were only a couple blocks away from my house now.

When we got there, I found Mouse waiting for me on the porch. "Beat you!" he said. He wasn't even breathing heavily. "That was really fast, wasn't it?"

"Uh, yeah, it was fast. Thanks." I took the box. It felt warm. I put it down, opened the top, and touched one of the chocolate bars. "Ouch!"

I yanked my hand back. "Hot?" Moose asked.

I nodded and sucked on my finger.

Moose poked one of the chocolate bars. The wrapper rippled like it was filled with liquid.  The chocolate bars were all melted.

"Quick! Put them in the fridge," Moose said.

"Good idea." I dragged the box inside. As I walked through the living room, I saw my little sister, Libby, and my older sister, Sarah Beth, playing with a large doll head.

"Where's the rest of that doll?" I asked.

"That's the whole thing," Sarah Beth said. "It's for trying out hairstyles."

"We are making pigtails," Libby said. "That's my favorite hairstyle because I love the story of the Three Little Pigs."

"Then you should make three pigtails," I joked.

I brought the box to the kitchen, grabbed an oven mitt, and started putting the chocolate bars in the fridge. Each bar drooped in my hands like an undercooked pancake.

Moose and Mouse gathered behind me. "I hope they aren't ruined," Mouse said.

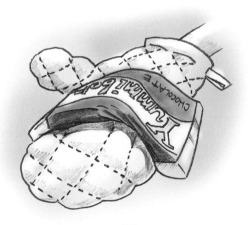

"Me too. If I can't sell them, I can't join the team. And I sure can't give them back to Mr. Netz like this. Not if I want him to think I can be responsible." I shut the door.

"I never knew I could go that fast," Mouse said. He turned toward his brother. "Want me to run your wrapping paper home?"

"No!" Moose said.

"Oink!" Mouse said.

No, wait. That wasn't Mouse.

"OINK! OINK!"

I looked under the kitchen table. There were pigs. Three little ones . . .

chapter 3

PIGS IN THE KITCHEN

"Cool!" Moose said. "One pig for each of us!" He didn't seem surprised, but I guess he was getting used to strange things happening around me.

"Where'd they come from?" Mouse asked.

I had a feeling I knew — especially since there was muddy straw, sticks, and bricks scattered under the table, too. I went to the living room.

"Look," Libby said, holding up the doll head. "We made three pigtails, just like you said."

And three pigs appeared out of nowhere, I thought. I pointed at the doll head.

"Where did you get that weird thing anyway?" I asked.

"Mom bought it for me at the New Curiosity Shop," Libby said.

That was Mr. Sage's store. It was full of strange and curious things. I had a feeling I should pay him a visit. But, right now, I had to get rid of these pigs.

"Hey," I said. "Pigtails are pretty easy. You should try something creative like . . ."

I searched my mind for a safe suggestion.

I was not exactly an expert on hairstyles. I thought about my friend Quentin Two. (I call him that because I have three friends named Quentin.) Sometimes, his mom braided his hair a special way. "Cornrows!" I shouted.

"Those would look cool," Sarah Beth said as she undid the pigtails.

With luck, my piggy problem was now solved. I returned to the kitchen. Yup — no pigs. That was a relief.

I heard Mom drive up. "Ed!" she called from outside. "Help me with the groceries!"

I went to the car. The air was even hotter now. I grabbed a bag from the trunk. Right on top, I saw a big green tray with six ears of corn, all in a row.

"That's strange. . . . I don't remember buying corn," Mom said.

She forgot all about the corn as soon as we got inside. She put her bag on the counter, then sniffed, frowned, and looked under the table. "Ed! You made a mess!"

"It wasn't me," I said. "It was the pigs!"

Mom glanced toward Moose and Mouse, then turned back toward me. "You shouldn't talk about your friends that way," she said.

"But . . ." I gave up trying to explain. I knew it was no use. I sighed and grabbed the mop.

Mom left the kitchen. Moose and Mouse stood there, laughing at me and making oinking sounds. I thought about saying "You really are pigs." But the idea that I might turn them into pigs, and maybe not be able to turn them back, scared me. So I kept my mouth shut.

After I cleaned the floor, I took one of the chocolate bars out of the fridge. It was hard again, but it wasn't flat. It was sort of warped.

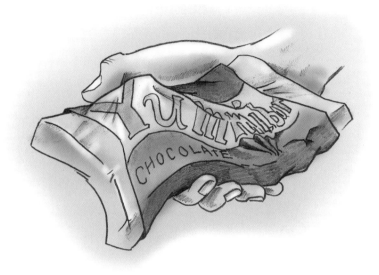

"I don't think I can sell these," I said.

"Maybe they still taste okay," Mouse said.

"Open one," Moose said. "That's the only way to tell."

My little brother, Derwin, walked into the kitchen. "Yeah, open it," he said.

I peeled back the foil, hoping to find a perfect chocolate bar. It wasn't pretty.

"I can't sell this," I said. "I'll bet I couldn't even give it away."

"I'll take it," Derwin said, snatching the bar from my hand. He broke off a piece and popped it in his mouth.

Normally, I would have grabbed it back from him. But I had a bigger problem. All the bars were ruined. I would have to pay for them myself if I wanted to play on the team. It looked like I simply had to come up with a money-making idea — and fast!

TURN UP THE HEAT

"Yay! Free chocolate!" Derwin said through gooey lips. "Now I've had two great things happen to me today."

"What are you talking about?" I asked.

"Remember what you told me this morning when you were walking me to school?" he asked.

I thought back to when Derwin had complained about the cold. I told him a funny quote our teacher had taught us the week before: **EVERYONE COMPLAINS ABOUT THE WEATHER, BUT NOBODY EVER DOES ANYTHING ABOUT IT.** "I remember," I said.

"Well, I don't like being cold," Derwin said. "So when I got home from school, *I* decided to do something about the weather."

Oh, no. I thought about the blazing heat. "What did you do?" I asked Derwin. *Or rather, what did I do?*

"Come on," he said, racing for the back door. "I'll show you!"

Derwin ran behind the garage. "See," he said, pointing to a large dial on the back wall. "We have one of these to change the temperature inside the house. I figured I could make one for outside, too. Right?"

"Uh, right . . ." I said. I tried to turn the dial, but it wouldn't move.

"Let me try," Mouse said. He started to twist the dial. I heard a cracking sound.

"Stop!" Derwin said. "You're breaking it!"

"Derwin, can you set it to 'comfort zone'?" I asked. It wouldn't surprise me if he was the only one who could turn the thermostat, since he was the one who made it.

"Sure," Derwin said. He turned the dial so the line pointed to COMFORT ZONE.

The air grew cooler. That was good. But I still had a fridge full of ugly chocolate bars to deal with. "I need to make money," I said. I checked my wallet. I had $6.00. That wasn't anywhere near enough to pay for thirty chocolate bars.

I walked back inside. Libby and Sarah Beth were styling the doll head again. "What are you making this time?" I asked.

"A ponytail," Libby said.

"No — don't!" I shouted, imagining the mess a pony would make. Even if the ponytail wasn't my suggestion, I didn't want to take any chances. Sometimes, strange things happened just because I was around.

They both stared at me. I said the first thing that came to mind: "You shouldn't spend all day indoors."

"But it's really hot," Sarah Beth said.

"Not anymore," I said.

"I don't want to go outside. I want to make the ponytail," Libby said.

"Here," I said, pulling a dollar from my wallet and handing it to Libby. "Get yourself an ice pop at the corner store."

"What about me?" Sarah Beth asked.

I sighed and gave her a dollar. That left me with $4.00.

I went to the kitchen, grabbed one of the chocolate bars from the fridge, and went outside. Moose, Mouse, and Derwin were in the driveway, playing soccer.

"Where are you going?" Moose asked.

"I think I know someone who'll buy the chocolate," I said. The idea had hit me when I was looking at the doll head. Mr. Sage sold all sorts of strange things. Maybe he'd buy my strange-looking chocolate and sell it to his customers. It was worth a try.

Besides, I had other things to talk to him about. Important things.

chapter 5

WHAT DID YOU SAY?

When I reached the shop, Mr. Sage was talking to a customer.

"Strange weather we've been having," the woman said as she paid for a sculpture of a monkey mummy made out of dried banana peels.

"Very strange," Mr. Sage said as he put the sculpture in a bag.

I waited until the woman left. Then I held up the Silver Center. "You told me things would get less strange once I gave this magic coin to the Stranger," I said.

"That was before we knew you were both the Finder and the Stranger," Mr. Sage said. "I don't believe that has ever happened before. There's no telling how strange things might get now that the coin is yours."

"No kidding. Look at this," I said, tossing the misshapen chocolate bar onto the counter. I tapped it. The bar was so warped, it wobbled back and forth like a tiny rocking horse.

"Oh, dear, that looks dreadful," he said. "Why did you bring it here?"

I explained how I'd told Mouse to go as fast as possible. "All the bars are like this. Any chance you'd buy them from me?"

He shook his head. "I'm afraid not. There is no way *I* could sell them."

"So what am I supposed to do?" I asked.

"I don't know," he said. "But what I *do* know is this — strangeness helps us be creative. And you certainly have no shortage of strangeness in your life. Use your power as the Stranger to find an answer to your problem. Wait! I do have something that might help you."

He strolled to the back of the shop, then returned and handed me a book.

"How can this help?" I asked.

"I've heard that each Stranger throughout history has discovered different abilities. From what you've told me, strange things often happen when you share quotes with other people," he said. "You might find ideas in this book."

He was right about the quotes. Look what had happened when I'd told Derwin that quote about the weather. Maybe the answer to my problem was in this book.

"Thanks," I said. I turned to leave, then looked back. "Hey, my mom bought my sister a doll head here. Was there anything strange about it?"

"Not until it got near you," Mr. Sage said, smiling.

"That's what I figured," I said.

As I headed out, I ran into Quentin One.

"I'm selling fruitcake to raise money for people who can't afford fruitcake," he said.

"Nobody wants fruitcake," I said.

"Everybody does," he said. "I only have one left. Want to buy it?"

"No thanks."

When I got home, I found Moose, Mouse, and Derwin in the backyard. They were all watching my cat, Willow, and my dog, Rex, chase each other in circles.

"Did you sell the chocolate to that weird guy?" Mouse asked.

"He wasn't interested. And, really, I can't blame him," I said. "What am I going to do?"

"Hey, remember how we found a dollar under that tree last week?" Derwin asked.

I definitely remembered that. Right after I became the Stranger, I'd said **"MONEY DOESN'T GROW ON TREES,"** and Derwin had decided maybe it grew under them. Sure enough, he found a dollar bill under the oak tree out front.

"Let's try it again!" Derwin said.

"Pick up the tree," I told Mouse.

Mouse gave Moose a funny look. Moose gave Mouse a funny look. And I got a funny feeling.

"What's wrong?" I asked.

At first, neither of them would answer me. Finally, Moose said, "Mouse and I went around to all the other trees the next day and picked up all the money."

"Where is it?" I asked. Maybe it was enough to pay for the chocolate.

"We spent it on jelly beans," Moose said.

"All of it?" I asked.

"Well, they were really, really good jelly beans," Mouse said. "Sorry."

I held up the book. "I guess we'll have to try something else," I said. "I'll bet the answer's in here. There have to be lots of quotes about money." My fingers tingled as I turned to the index in the back of the book. . . .

chapter 6

MONEY HUNT

I found the section on money and started reading quotes aloud. **"A FOOL AND HIS MONEY ARE SOON PARTED."** I guess that meant careless people spend their money quickly.

"A fool and his chocolate are soon melted," Moose said. He grinned.

I ignored him and read the next one. **"A PENNY IS A LOT OF MONEY IF YOU DON'T HAVE A PENNY."** That was true but it didn't seem like it would help. I tried another: **"MONEY TALKS."** I guess that meant, if you had money, you could get things done.

"Money talks!" Moose said. "Maybe we can hear it. And if we can hear it, we can find it! People are always losing money."

"Yeah," Derwin said. "Let's listen." He cupped his left hand behind his ear.

"This won't work," I said.

"Shhhh!" Derwin said. "Wait! I hear something." He skittered down the street. "Gotcha!" he shouted, snatching something from the grass.

"What did you find?" I asked when I caught up with him.

Derwin handed me a penny. "Hey, now I hear another one," he said. He dashed ahead of us, plucked something from the sidewalk, and tossed me a quarter.

I jiggled the coins in my hands and listened to the clinks they made. *Money talks*, I thought. I guess I'd made it talk. Maybe I'd finally used my power to solve my problem.

I held the coins near my ear. Lincoln and Washington were arguing about who was more honest.

I followed Derwin down the street as he discovered three more pennies, but no more quarters. By then, we'd covered eight blocks.

"This isn't going to work," I said. "If we find one coin at a time, it will take months to make enough money. I have to turn in my chocolate money next week."

"We'll think of something," Moose said. He tapped his watch. "But it will have to be tomorrow. Mouse and I need to get home. We want to watch Dad cut the cheese."

"What?" I asked.

"It's his new hobby," Mouse explained. "He's been making all sorts of cheeses. Half the fridge is filled with milk."

Then they headed off. And I walked back home with Derwin, who found two more pennies on the way. All the Lincolns were drowning out the lonely Washington.

Right before we reached home, we ran into Quentin Two.

Quentin Two

"I'm raising money to buy sneakers for the chess club," he said, holding up a loaf of bread and a package of cheese.

"What is that?" I asked.

"A grilled-cheese sandwich kit," he said. "Want one?"

"No thanks. But I will chip in for some shoelaces." I handed him the loose coins we'd found, then went inside.

Maybe I shouldn't look only at money quotes. I wondered what else was in the book. I flipped it open and scanned a page.

DON'T LOOK A GIFT HORSE IN THE MOUTH.

Dad told me that people check a horse's teeth before they buy it, to make sure it's in good condition and worth the price. I guess this saying means, if you get a gift, you shouldn't worry about how good it is.

There were more horse quotes, but I stopped reading because an idea hit me that was so awesome I let out a shout.

"Got it!"

I ran outside to find Libby and Sarah Beth.

"You need to make that ponytail now," I said.

I had it all figured out. I'd
go around the neighborhood,
selling pony rides. People paid a
lot for a pony ride at the carnival.
I could make all the money I
needed — and more — in no time.

"We don't feel like doing hair anymore," Libby said.

"I'll give you another dollar," I said.

"Each of us?" Sarah Beth asked.

"All right, each of you," I said. I gave them the money. Then, with only $2.00 left in my wallet, I followed them into the house.

Sarah Beth undid the cornrows. Then she brushed the doll's hair, pulling it back. After she gathered it, she slipped a rubber band around it and put the hair in a little ponytail.

I hope this works, I thought.

A second later, I heard a neighing from the kitchen. I ran there as quickly as I could!

chapter 7

A PONY TALE

There was a pony in the kitchen, right where the pigs had been. Yup — it was standing *under* the table. And it wasn't in any danger of bumping its head. It was the smallest pony I'd ever seen. No one would be riding it.

I had to get it out of the kitchen before it made a stinky mess. I opened the back door. "Come on. Scat! Scoot!"

It stared at me and blinked.

"Giddyup!" I shouted.

That didn't work, either.

I heard Mom coming down the hall toward the kitchen. "Have you seen the corn?" she called. "It seems to have disappeared."

I ran back to the living room. "Comb out the ponytail," I said. "Right now!"

"You're mister bossy pants today," Libby said.

"We like the ponytail," Sarah Beth said. She put her hands on her hips and glared at me.

I yanked out my wallet and grabbed my last two dollars. "Here. Okay?" I asked.

"Okay," they said.

"Let me know when you want us to make something else," Sarah Beth said.

"I can't afford anything else!" I shouted.

They combed out the ponytail. I went back to the kitchen just in time to get in trouble with Mom. That pony might have been the size of a dog, but it sure wasn't trained like one. I went to get the mop.

That night, I sat on my bed and flipped through the quote book. I didn't see anything that might help me make money.

I put down the book and picked up the Silver Center. "Is there a strange solution to my problem?" I asked it.

Unlike the coins Derwin had found, my coin remained silent. But outside my window, for just a moment, the moon seemed to twinkle like a star.

"Read me a story," Libby said, breaking into my thoughts.

I had to be careful. Whatever story I read to Libby at night seemed to happen for real the next day.

"Goldilocks . . ." I said to myself. "Gold . . ."
I knew that even a little bit of gold was worth
a lot of money. I wondered whether I could
tell Libby a story about a girl with golden
hair. It was worth a try.

I just had to be sure to leave out the part
about the bears. It was bad enough cleaning
up after the pigs and the pony.

"I know an even better story," I told her as
I followed her to her room.

After we got settled, I made up a story about a girl whose hair turns to gold. I made sure to describe her so she looked like the doll head. I didn't want anything to happen to Libby's or Sarah Beth's hair.

"I hope this works," I said as I climbed back into my own bed.

chapter 8

GRAB THAT GOLD!

The next morning, I was awakened by voices from downstairs.

"Her hair is so stiff today," Libby said.

"It's wiry," Sarah Beth said. "But so shiny. I don't remember it being this shiny."

Stiff? Wiry? Shiny? I sat straight up and felt my heart racing. Maybe the doll head's hair had turned to gold just like I'd wanted it to! This was awesome. I was saved. I was about to run downstairs when the phone rang.

I picked it up. "Hello?"

"I figured out how to make money," Moose said.

"That's great," I said. "But I think I solved everything."

"I hope you didn't come up with some sort of harebrained idea," Moose said.

"Not exactly," I said.

"Well, give me a call if you change your mind," Moose said. "I have a ton of free time. I already sold all my wrapping paper."

"That's great." I hung up the phone and went downstairs to the living room.

Sarah Beth was trimming the doll head's hair. I almost gasped when I saw all that shiny gold.

"You're giving her a haircut?" I asked.

"No, it's just a trim," Sarah Beth said.

That was perfect. I could sell the clippings. "It looks like you're giving her bangs," I said. I turned away, figuring I'd come back for the clippings after they were finished. But I didn't get very far. A jumble of images tumbled through my brain.

They'd made pigtails, and pigs appeared.

They'd made cornrows, and corn appeared.

They'd made a ponytail, and a pony appeared.

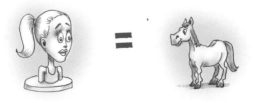

Now they were making bangs.

Bangs...

"Look out!" I shouted. I raced over and snatched up the doll head. The hair over its forehead had started to glow and sizzle, like lit fuses.

"Duck!" I screamed as I hurled the head at the window. It smashed through the glass, landed on the lawn, rolled halfway to the street, and exploded.

All three of us ran to the window. There was a small crater on the lawn, and no sign of the doll head . . . or the gold.

From behind me, I heard Dad come up from his workshop in the basement. "Ed," he said, "how many times have I warned you about playing ball in the house? You're paying for that window, young man!"

"I don't suppose I can pay in chocolate bars," I muttered. I went outside and kicked dirt back into the crater so Dad wouldn't notice it. Then I headed to Moose's house. I figured, whatever his plan was, it would be safer than any of mine.

chapter 9

SQUEEZE!

A block later, I ran into Quentin Three. "I'm selling doorknobs to raise money for the Children's Theater production of *Winnie the Pooh Meets Godzilla.* I'm playing Eeyore."

"Uhhh . . . good luck," I said.

I kept walking, and I tried to think of any other way I could make money. *I guess I could mop floors,* I thought. I'd sure gotten a lot of experience doing that recently. But I had a feeling nobody else in the neighborhood had the sort of messes I had.

"My plan blew up," I told Moose when I got to his house. "What's your idea?"

"We sell ice-cold glasses of orange juice," he said.

"Where are we going to get oranges?" I asked.

Moose pointed to his brother, Mouse. "From me," Mouse said. "I have to sell oranges for my class trip, so I have a lot of them."

"But I don't have money for oranges," I said. "I don't have any money at all."

"That's okay," Mouse said. "You can pay me *after* you sell the juice."

This didn't sound like a great idea. It sounded like a way for me to lose even more money. "I don't think we can possibly sell enough juice for this to work," I said.

"We can sell a whole bunch if it gets real hot again," Moose said.

"But how can . . ." I stopped as I realized that Moose was referring to Derwin's outdoor thermostat. "Let's do it!"

We ran inside. Moose grabbed a pitcher, and then Mouse grabbed an orange.

"Squeeze hard," I said. "We want lots of juice."

Mouse gave the orange a hard squeeze. Too hard. Moose and I hit the floor as a spray of seeds shot from the orange. I heard a crash as some seeds broke the kitchen window.

Moose and Mouse looked at me. It wasn't *exactly* my fault, but by this point, it didn't matter. "I'll pay for the window," I said. "But this better work."

Moose and I squeezed a bunch of Mouse's oranges — carefully — while Mouse set up a table and a sign in their front yard.

After that, I called Derwin.

"Turn up your thermostat," I said.

"But you said I shouldn't mess with the weather," he said.

"Just this once," I said. "Please."

"Okay," he said, hanging up the phone.

I looked at all the people walking past. In a moment, the sun would glare down on them, and they'd all get super thirsty.

Next to me, Moose shivered.

Then Mouse folded his arms around himself and said, "Brrrr."

"Is it getting cold?" I asked.

"It seems to be," Moose said.

I looked up as a snowflake landed on my nose. A chill ran down my back, and it wasn't just from the air temperature. The chill came from knowing I was in big trouble.

chapter 10

SWEET SOLUTION

I called Derwin. "You turned it the wrong way!" I told him. I realized I should have given him better directions than telling him to turn it up. "Turn it the other way. Hurry!"

I heard the sound of him running. Then I heard a grunt, followed by a snap.

Oh no! The dial had broken. I was shivering now. A freezing blast of wind tore our sign away and nearly lifted our table. I could see bits of ice forming in the pitcher of juice.

I'd failed. It was all over. I could forget about being on the soccer team. I owed money for the team's chocolate bars, for my parents' window, for Moose and Mouse's parents' window, and for Mouse's oranges. I'd be working for the rest of my life to pay people back. There was no hope.

But then I thought of a quote that Mom said all the time.

WHEN LIFE GIVES YOU LEMONS, MAKE LEMONADE.

She had explained it meant that when something bad happens, you need to turn it into something good. Well, life had given me melted chocolate. And thinking about melted chocolate gave me an idea.

"Mouse," I said, "can you run to my house and get the chocolate from my fridge?"

"Sure," he said.

"Use the empty box in my room," I said.
"Go as fast as possible!"

"I'm on it!" He flashed away.

"Are you out of your mind?" Moose said. "That's how all of this started."

"And that is how we're going to fix *everything*," I said. "Come on! Let's get some milk."

Moose looked like he was about to argue, but then I could tell that he realized what I had in mind. "Brilliant!" he said.

We ran inside his house and grabbed what we needed. Since Moose's dad's new hobby was making cheese, there was plenty of milk in his fridge.

By the time we got back out to our table, Mouse was waiting for us with a big box full of super-heated chocolate.

I handed Mouse a gallon of milk. "Run around the block. Go as fast as possible!"

ZOOM!
BOOM!

I mixed the super-heated melted chocolate with the scalding-hot milk.

"Hot chocolate!" I shouted to the passing crowd as the wonderful aroma filled the air.

The mob surged toward us, eager for a hot treat on a freezing day. They bought every single drop.

I smiled as I realized that I'd used my problem — melted chocolate — to solve my problem.

I made enough money to cover everything. I gave Mouse money for the oranges, the milk, and the window, then counted out what I needed for the chocolate bars and for my parents' window. I already knew exactly how much a window cost, since I'd broken one or two in the past. Or maybe it was three. Okay, it was four.

I even had $6.00 left over for myself. I was back where I'd started. Happily, the weather returned to normal as soon as Derwin took down the broken thermostat.

On the way home, I swung past the New Curiosity Shop. "Do you have another doll head?" I asked Mr. Sage. "I sort of owe my sisters a present."

He spread his empty hands. "Alas, it was one of a kind. But if you would like to replace it, I have all sorts of interesting gifts."

"I only have six dollars," I said.

"That's exactly what the best ones cost," he said, giving me a wink.

I wasn't surprised. Not much surprises me these days. After all, I am the Stranger. But that's not *all* I am. Next week, once I turned in my chocolate money, I'd become a responsible member of the soccer team. And there's nothing strange about that!

Check out
the next
LOONIVERSE book!

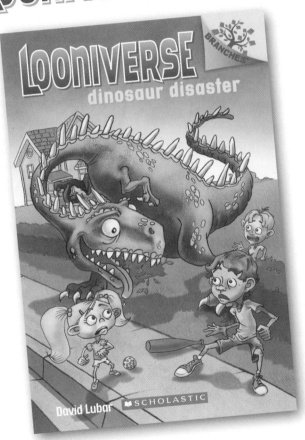

DAVID LUBAR loves writing weird and funny books, such as *Attack of the Vampire Weenies: And Other Weird and Creepy Tales*. He has never traveled anywhere near as fast as the speed of light. But he especially enjoys exploring all the strange events that can happen in the Looniverse. He lives in Nazareth, PA. If you come to his door there selling things for your team, he'll always choose chocolate over wrapping paper.

MATT LOVERIDGE loves drawing and painting the many wacky things that happen in the Looniverse. He especially loves illustrating all the animal messes! Matt lives in Pleasant Grove, Utah, with his wife and children. Luckily, the only wild animals that he has to clean up after are his five kids and their dog, Blue.